GROLIER

Your partner in education

**Distributed by Grolier, Sherman Turnpike
Danbury, Connecticut 06816**

Grolier offers a varied selection of
children's book racks and tote bags.
For details on ordering, please write:
Grolier Direct Marketing
Sherman Turnpike
Danbury, CT 06816
Att: Premium Department

My Book

by Jane Belk Moncure

illustrated by Vera Gohman

THE CHILD'S WORLD

Mankato, MN 56001

Little  had a box.

"I will fill my  box," she said.

Little went skip, skip,

skip up a hill.

She found inchworms,

lots of little
inchworms.

The inchworms wiggled
and wiggled.

"What wiggly
inchworms," she said.

She put the
inchworms
into her box.

Then Little **i** found iguanas,

lots of iguanas.

The iguanas wiggled.

"What wiggly iguanas," she said.

She put the iguanas

into the box with the inchworms.

The inchworms were not happy.

Out they jumped.

The iguanas jumped out too.

Away they went.

Little i could not find the inchworms or

the
iguanas.

They were hiding.

Then Little

found an igloo.

She put the igloo into her box.

But the sun came out.

Guess what.

The igloo melted.

"Who will help me
fill my box?" she said.

An Indian came by.

"I will help you
fill your box," she said.

The Indian found
an Indian dress,

Indian moccasins,

Indian beads,

an Indian drum,

and an Indian headband.

Guess where they put
the Indian things.

"Thank you," said Little .

"Now I will dress like an Indian!"

And she did!

inchworms

Indian

iguana

More words with Little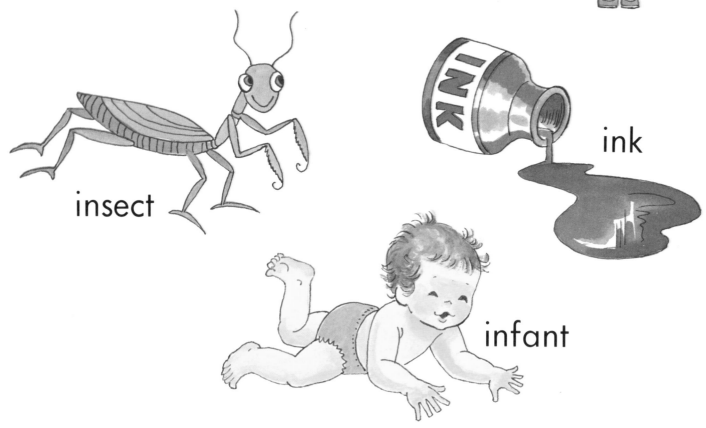

insect

ink

infant

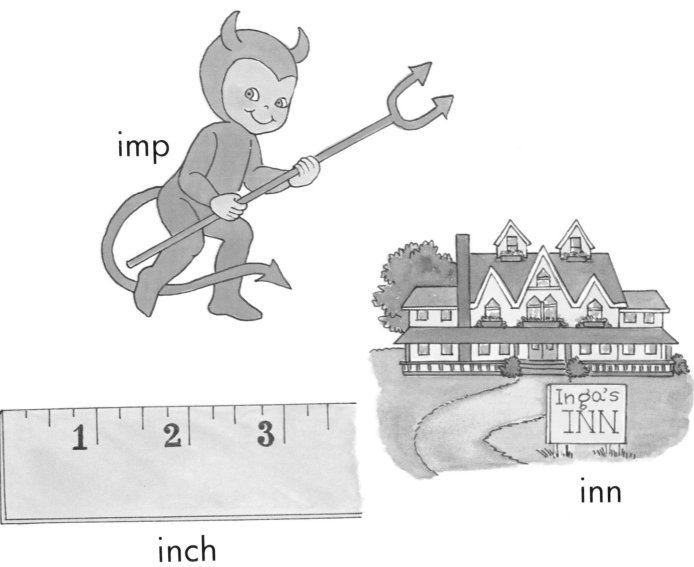

imp

inch

inn